JACOB'S GIFT

For Allen and Maria Dutton,

your children and grandchildren—

Because you love Jesus.

Because you love Brazil.

And because you've loved us.

Text copyright © 1998 by Max Lucado.
Illustrations copyright © 1998 by Robert Hunt.

Published in Nashville, Tennessee, by Tommy Nelson™,
a division of Thomas Nelson, Inc. Executive Editor: Laura Minchew.

Library of Congress Cataloging-in-Publication Data
Lucado, Max.
    Jacob's gift / Max Lucado : illustrated by Robert Hunt.
      p. cm.
    Summary: A young carpenter's apprentice works very hard on
his woodworking project, only to give it away to a special baby.
    ISBN 0-8499-5830-X
    1. Jesus Christ—Nativity—Juvenile fiction. [1. Jesus Christ—
Nativity—Fiction. 2. Carpenters Fiction.] I. Hunt, Robert,
1952– ill. II. Title.
PZ7.L9684Jac 1998
[E] dc21   98–6490
                                                       CIP
                                                       AC

Printed in the United States of America
98 99 00 01 02 LBM 9 8 7 6 5 4 3 2 1

JACOB'S GIFT

Max Lucado

Illustrated by
ROBERT HUNT

Tommy
NELSON

Thomas Nelson, Inc.
Nashville

Rabbi Simeon brushed the sawdust off his hands and began untying his apron. "Before you leave today, I have a special announcement." He hung the apron on a wooden peg and turned to look at the handful of boys in his shop. All but one apprentice had removed their aprons and put away their tools.

Rabbi Simeon looked across the workshop. One boy continued sawing a piece of wood.

"Jacob," the rabbi instructed, "our work is finished for the day. Put away your tools."

Jacob didn't respond. The only sound he heard was the *swish-swish* of the saw. And now, *swish-swish* was the only sound anyone heard. But Jacob didn't know that. The other boys in the shop began to snicker.

Rabbi Simeon let out a deep sigh and shook his head, but he wasn't mad. Down deep he was pleased. He, too, knew what it was like to get lost in the world of woodworking. But it was time to go home.

"Jacob!" the rabbi called again, his voice a bit louder this time.

The sawing stopped. When Jacob heard no other noise, he knew he'd done it again. Slowly he placed his saw on the table.

"I'm sorry, Rabbi," he said softly.

Rabbi Simeon smiled. "It's all right. Put away your tools and hang up your apron."

Jacob quickly cleaned off his work area. With a sigh he stood and walked across the room, never looking up. This was the part he hated most. Everyone was looking at him. He hung up his apron as the other boys continued to snicker. Jacob's cheeks burned. Finally the rabbi spoke, and all eyes turned back to him.

"As I said earlier, my nephew from Nazareth should be here within a few days. He is a master carpenter who knows quality work. He will help me select one of you for a special task. The one who builds the best project will work with me on the new synagogue."

It will be me! The words were so strong in Jacob's thoughts, he feared he had spoken them out loud. Only days earlier he'd overheard the rabbi say, "Just leave Jacob alone with wood and he can do almost anything." Jacob had turned red then, too, but that time with pride.

I just have to be chosen, Jacob determined. *I want to use my hands to help build God's house. It doesn't matter that everyone says I'm so shy. This time . . .*

"Jacob, did you hear what I said?"

"Uh . . . no, sir."

"I'll be away for the next three days, but you may all use the workshop to finish your projects." As the others began to leave, the rabbi asked Jacob to stay.

Again, Jacob felt his cheeks warm. He waited till everyone had left and then approached the carpenter.

"I'm sorry, Rabbi," he apologized. "I'll do better next time."

The rabbi motioned for Jacob to sit on one of the stools. "Oh, Jacob, you've done nothing wrong. I asked you to stay so I could tell you something." The rabbi smiled, pulled up a stool, and sat down. He placed his big hand on Jacob's shoulder and began. "God has given you the gift of woodworking. What is difficult for many is easy for you. Surely, you've noticed."

Jacob nodded slowly. He had wondered why other boys struggled with the wood to make things that seemed so simple to him.

"God gives gifts, Jacob. Some can sing, others teach, and you — you can build. You have a special gift. Have you ever wondered why God gave you this gift?"

"So I can learn to be a good carpenter?" he guessed.

"Well," the rabbi chuckled, "not exactly. God gave you this gift to share with others. Let's say you gave a present to one of my daughters. How do you think that would make me feel?"

"Happy?"

"Of course. Even though you gave the gift to my child, I would feel like you had given it to me. God is like that, too. When we give a gift to one of His children, it's like giving a gift to God. If you ever have a chance to help somebody, remember what I told you.

"Now, run home and tell your father that I hope he has an inn full of guests next week."

That evening at supper Jacob's father reminded him of the days ahead. "We're expecting a lot of business, son."

"I'll get up early," promised Jacob. "I will work on my project in the mornings and help you in the evenings."

The next three mornings Jacob crawled out of bed while it was still dark and went to the workshop. With a fire going and a lamp burning, he worked hard to complete his project. The other boys had laughed when he told them what he was going to build, but now that it was almost finished, they weren't laughing anymore.

Jacob was building a new kind of animal feed trough. His would have wheels. He got the idea while watching some men work in the stable next to his father's inn. They loaded a wagon full of hay, rolled it into the shed, and dumped it in the trough. He thought, *Why not put wheels on the trough?* And that's what Jacob was planning to do.

Jacob had returned to the workshop after helping his father at the inn. *Rabbi Simeon will be here tomorrow; I must finish tonight,* thought the sleepy boy. Jacob looked at the trough and then at the four wheels piled on his workbench. *So much work still to do.* He was so tired. *Maybe if I close my eyes for a few minutes . . .*

In what seemed like the very next moment, a beam of starlight slipped through a crack and fell across Jacob's napping eyes. "What!" he shouted, startled by the sudden light. Had he slept through the night? Then he looked out and saw the village showered by a gleaming, shimmering light in the night.

Jacob rubbed the sleep from his eyes as he walked outside and toward the star that seemed to dance in the sky near his father's inn.

Then he heard a strange sound in the stable behind the inn. Quietly, Jacob crept closer. He looked through a knothole in the stable wall. There, in a tiny nest of straw on the ground, was a baby! Beside the baby knelt his mother. A man gently covered her with his cloak. *The baby must be uncomfortable on the ground,* Jacob thought.

Quickly, Jacob turned and raced back to the workshop. He stood beside his newly built feed trough. He had measured each board so carefully. He had cut each piece with skill. He had oiled it with care. It was the best work Jacob had ever done. Tomorrow the rabbi would select the best apprentice.

But tonight there's a new baby without a place to sleep....

"Good morning, boys," said Rabbi Simeon. "This is the big day."

Jacob approached the rabbi. "Uh, sir . . . I need to tell you something."

"Later, Jacob. We need to get everything ready for my nephew. Here, help me." The rabbi's voice drifted off as he began to take the projects outside—an unfinished chair, a desk with one leg too short, and a wobbly stool. Then, looking at a stack of four wheels, he asked, "Where is your project, Jacob?"

"That's what I tried to tell you. Something happened. There was this big star and—"

"Uncle Simeon!"

"Joseph!" Simeon shouted, extending his arms. "I'm so glad you're here!"

Jacob's eyes widened. This was the man he had seen with the baby in the stable the night before. With one arm still around Joseph, the rabbi turned to Jacob.

"Jacob, this is my nephew from Nazareth."

Jacob was too surprised to speak, so Joseph spoke in his place. "We've already met," said Joseph, putting a hand on the boy's shoulder. "In fact, Jacob gave my newborn son his very first gift."

"Your son?" the rabbi inquired. "What son? Where is he?"

"Come, and I'll show you."

And the rabbi and Jacob hurried behind Joseph.

Joseph led them around a curve and down a hill toward the inn. "Did you stay at the inn, Joseph?"

"Not quite, it was too full." Joseph smiled.

"Then where did you stay?" asked Rabbi Simeon.

"You'll see." Joseph led them past the inn to the bottom of the hill. There he left the path and turned toward a shelter. "The stable?" Simeon asked. "You kept your baby in a—"

Joseph smiled and placed a finger to his lips, "Quiet, Uncle. They're asleep. Follow me." He lowered his head and entered the stable.

A cow mooed at the presence of the trio. Joseph stepped next to the trough and motioned for them to approach. When the rabbi and his student looked inside, they saw a beautiful newborn baby.

"His name is Jesus," Joseph whispered. "And he has a cradle fit for a king."

Joseph's kindness made Jacob's cheeks turn red. But he felt so good, seeing the baby asleep in the feed trough he had made.

"Now I see why your project was missing," said the rabbi, "and it is the finest project I've seen. You will be the one to help build God's house. But, tell me, why did you decide to give your feed trough away?"

Jacob smiled with delight.

"I remembered what you said, Rabbi. 'When you give a gift to one of God's children, you give a gift to God,'" said the boy.

The rabbi's voice was soft. "And so you have, my son. So you have."